Lo

&

Found

Jean Lauzier

White Bird Publications
P.O Box 90145
Austin, Texas   778709
www.whitebirdpublications.com

ISBN: 978-1-63363-379-7
LCCN: 2019933731

PRINTED IN THE UNITED STATES OF AMERICA.

To my daughter, Rebekah. Thanks so much for watching the Heathen while I'm away. I really appreciate it.

Lost & Found

White Bird
Publications

Chapter One

JoAnne Mathis placed the metal feed pan on the shelf and leaned on the half-door and studied the seven Belgian Malinois puppies playing within. She grinned when purple-collar boy growled as his littermates tried to steal his tug. He had a firm grip on the cloth toy and wasn't going to let go. At six weeks old, biting was something they did well. Jo had the marks to prove it. Purple-collar boy would be the one she'd choose—if Mom would let her. Jo sighed. She'd begged for over a year for her own pup until Mom finally told her it wasn't going to happen. At least not until Jo earned the right to have one. Thing was, Mom wouldn't say what it would take to earn one.

At least, for a few days, she could pretend. Mom had gone to some training symposium and left Jo behind. Behind to feed the dogs, clean up the poop, and make sure every dog had time in the main play yard. Then repeat the feeding and cleaning again in the afternoon.

A nose nudged the pocket of her hoodie. Ziva, a five-year-old Belgian Malinois, momma to the nearby puppies, nosed the pocket again. Jo scratched behind Ziva's fuzzy ears then pulled a bit of dried beef from the pocket.

"Here you go, girl."

Ziva scarfed the treat then barked softly.

"Nope, no more for you. You don't want to get fat now, do you?"

Jo rested her arms on top of the door again and whistled softly. Purple-collar boy whirled around and barked. Yep, he'd definitely be the one she'd pick.

"I figured I'd find you here." Diego strode down the center aisle toward her. "Don't you think it's time you get serious and stop playing around?" He halted beside Jo and gave Ziva a pat. "Your mom may not be here, but work still needs to get done. I shouldn't have to come looking for you or go behind you to make sure everything gets done." Diego shook his head. "I've got to go pick up a rescue. I'll be gone most of the day. You need to step up and act like an adult." He started back the way he'd come but stopped and looked at her. "Don't make me regret leaving you here alone." He shrugged and disappeared around the corner.

Jo sighed and checked her watch. Only eight o'clock. How she'd love to sleep in on a Saturday morning. She picked up the metal feed pan and patted her leg. "Come on, Ziva. Time for work."

Back in the main kennel, she collected the breakfast pans and carried them to the kitchen. Mom insisted they be hand washed, so Jo piled them in the sink, added dish soap, and turned on the hot water. She'd let the pans soak while she cleaned the kennels. Mom had taken Rex with her, so there were only five runs to clean. Still, it was Jo's least favorite chore.

A large black cat strolled into the kitchen and meowed. BC rubbed against Jo's leg. She picked him up. "Good morning to you. Kill anything last night?" BC just purred as she rubbed his tummy. Jo wasn't normally a cat person, but BC was different. Not only did he like to be around people, but he wasn't afraid of any dogs. In fact, the dogs soon learned to respect and leave him alone. She hadn't expected Mom to take her suggestion to name the kennel after the cat, but apparently, it amused her mom too. Jo set him on the counter and added fresh kibble to his dish. "There you go. Eat up."

The dogs barked when she entered the kennel side

of the building. "Yeah, yeah, yeah. I know. Y'all want to go out." She strode down the aisle letting the dogs out of their runs and led them to the main exercise yard outside. Thankfully, they all got along so could play together. She closed the gate behind them and turned back to the kennels.

Inside, she cleaned each kennel then gathered up the water buckets and carried them to the kitchen. It didn't take long to get the feed pans washed and stacked. The water buckets, she washed then carried back to the kennels and filled them with fresh water.

She checked her watch. Only nine. She'd made good time this morning. The dogs still had at least an hour in the yard, so Jo hurried to the kennel office and settled in at the desk. While the computer was starting, Jo flipped through her DVDs. She picked a puppy training DVD and inserted it into the disk drive. One day she would have a pup of her own, and she planned to be ready.

The phone in her pocket vibrated. She checked at

the screen. And unknown number. The phone vibrated again, so she answered.

" Black Cat Kennels." Normally she'd not answer an unknown number but with Mom away, no telling who might be calling. She listened as the caller identified himself as Sheriff Porter. He didn't call often, but when he did, it was serious. Jo took a deep breath. "What can I do for you, Sheriff?"

"I need one of your tracking dogs. Oak Hollow Assisted Living Center called, and one of their residents is missing."

"What's the address?" She scribbled the details on a scrap of paper then repeated it back. "Got it. I'll send Diego right over."

Jo shoved the phone in her pocket, grabbed the note she'd written, and rushed to the door. Soon as she touched the doorknob, she remembered.

Diego had left and wouldn't be back for hours.

Chapter Two

Jo glanced at the paper in her hand. Assisted living meant it was an elderly person missing. She paced across the office. Should she call Diego and have him come back? It'd be at least an hour before he could get here. And even if she had everything ready for him, it'd take too long. She took a deep breath, then hurried to the exercise yard. There, she studied the dogs within.

Ziva had a darn good nose, but it had been a while

since she'd worked a track. Jazz and Xena hadn't even been started tracking yet. That left Tango and Taz. Taz might be the better tracker, but he had a wild streak that sometimes made him unreliable. Tango it would be.

"Let's go, guys. Playtime's over." Jo returned the others to their kennels then headed to the ready room with Tango at her side.

Mom always liked to be prepared, so Jo grabbed a backpack from the shelf and slung it over her shoulder.

Back in the office, she left a note for Diego, snagged a leash from the hook by the door, and headed to the Jeep.

Jo parked near the rear of the parking lot of Oak Hollow Assisted Living Center. The lot almost overflowed with vehicles. Two patrol cars, a sheriff's SUV, and a local radio station van were parked up front. Tango stood in the passenger seat, barked once, then sat.

"You wait here. I'll be right back." Jo patted Tango's side then stepped out of her Jeep, locked the door, and headed toward the main building.

In the lobby stood a group made up of police officers, Oak Hollow staff, and what looked to be members of a search party. She greeted the nearest officer and asked if he knew where Sheriff Porter could be found.

He nodded. "He's in the dining room. It's being used as our command center. May I help you with something?"

"Can you let him know that his tracking dog is here?"

"Sorry." He held out his hand. "I'm Brad Thompson. Ted told me to watch for you, but I wasn't expecting a female or a teenager.'

"No problem. Happens all the time."

"Ted said to find him soon as you got here." He

waved toward a hallway. "The dining room is this way."

They strolled down the hall until Officer Thompson opened a door then stepped aside. "Here we are."

A group of men stood around a small table. A tall man in uniform turned toward her and frowned. He spoke to the men then headed toward her.

Jo straightened her shoulders and tried to stand taller. She could do this.

"Where's Diego?" Sheriff Porter gazed down at her. "I need to get him started asap."

"He's on the road to get a rescue. It'd take too long for him to get here." She swallowed hard. "I can do this. I've helped Mom and Diego train, and I brought the same dog Diego would have."

Sheriff Porter glanced back at the group gathered around the table then at Jo. He leaned in and lowered his voice. "Have you ever done this off a training field?"

Jo shook her head. "No, but I..."

The sheriff held up his hand. "If anyone asks, you do this all the time. You understand?"

Jo nodded.

"Then let's go."

They strode back to the table. "Folks, this is Jo Mathis. She has some of the best tracking dogs I've ever worked with." Polite hellos and nods greeted her. "We're getting familiar with the immediate area." He tapped a spot on the map. "We're here. The building and the immediate grounds have been searched. There are several walking trails that go into the woods though. We left those for you."

"Good. The less people on them the better."

Sheriff Porter pointed to a spot on the map. "This is the closest trail, but we'll see what your dog says."

Jo nodded. "I'll get Tango and meet you out front. Do you have something that belongs to the missing person? And just who are we looking for?"

Sheriff Porter pulled out a small notebook, flipped

it open. "Frank Hawthorne, age 86. Caucasian male. He's in good physical health but is dealing with the beginnings of dementia." He returned the notebook to his pocket then pulled a picture from a stack of papers on the table. "This was taken not long ago. I'll have one of the staff grab a shirt or something of his."

"Okay. Let's get going." Jo hurried across the parking lot. At her Jeep, she grabbed her backpack, slung it over her shoulder, then snapped a leash on Tango's collar. Tango licked her face. Jo took his head in her hands and looked him in the eyes. "We may not be the "A-team," but we can do this."

Tango jumped from the driver's seat then watered the nearest shrub while Jo closed the car door.

"All right, Tango. Let's go."

They hurried across the parking lot toward the main building. Right up front, a beige Caddy took up two handicapped parking spaces. Jo shook her head. "Wonder what they're over-compensating for." She glanced around. "Now where is Sheriff Porter?" Jo found him inside the building. An angry blonde stood in front of him, poking him in the chest with a silver clutch.

"If something happens to my father, I'll have your badge." She poked him again. "And I'll own this place and fire everyone who works here."

Sheriff Porter stepped back. "Mrs. Peters, as I told you, we've searched the entire facility and grounds." He nodded toward Jo. "I've got a tracking dog ready to search, so if you'll excuse me, I'll get on that."

The woman turned and stared at Jo then gazed down at Tango and frowned. "That's a skinny German Shepherd. It is sick or something?" She looked back at the sheriff. "This is the best you can do? Some local kid and her sick dog?"

Jo took a deep breath. "He's not a German Shepherd. He's a Belgian Malinois."

The blonde faced Jo. "I don't care what it is. I'm calling my attorney and telling him about this fiasco."

"Tiffany! That's enough."

Tiffany huffed out a breath and crossed her arms in front of her chest as a tall, blond man in a suit joined them. "I apologize for my sister. He held his hand out to the sheriff. "I'm Mark Hawthorne. I think we spoke this morning. Thank you for all your help." Mark looked at Jo. "And thank you too. I appreciate you coming out."

"Markie, they lost Daddy. And they aren't doing anything. He's been out there for hours. He could be hurt, and they are just standing around running their mouths." Tiffany shifted her clutch from one hand to the other. "I'm so worried about him."

"Then let them do their job and quit distracting them." Mark nodded at Sheriff Porter. "How can I help, Sherriff?"

"We're about to start the dog. Just give us some room and time." Sheriff Porter took a step toward the door. "Let's go, Jo."

At the door, Jo halted and glanced back at Tiffany. "Ma'am, is that your Caddy parked out front?"

Tiffany nodded. "It is. Why do you want to know?"

"You're parked in two handicap spaces without a permit. If I were you, I'd move your car before you get a ticket."

"They wouldn't dare."

"Up to you." Jo shrugged and followed the sheriff out the door.

"Oh, I will dare." He waved over an officer who stood with a group of Oak Hollow staff. "See that Caddy over there?"

The officer glanced toward the car then back at Sheriff Porter. "Yes, sir. It's parked illegally, so I ticketed it. I can take it off and let it go if you want."

Sheriff Porter grinned. "No, it's good. Thanks."

Jo and Tango followed the sheriff to a bench that sat under an old oak. He handed her a handheld radio then pulled a red t-shirt from a plastic bag and handed it to Jo. "This is the shirt he wore yesterday."

"Perfect." She unfastened Tango's leash and held

the shirt in front of him. After he took several deeps sniffs, he looked up at her and whined. "Good boy, Tango. Go find."

Chapter Three

A small courtyard filled with flowers occupied the area next to the front entrance of Oak Hollow. There were umbrella-shaded tables, wrought-iron benches, and a fountain with an elephant spraying water in the midst of potted plants. Tango raced around the fountain and past a bench then came to a sudden halt. Lowering his nose to the ground, his tail swept from side to side as he slowly followed the invisible scent trail through the courtyard.

"Sheriff Porter, may I have a word with you?" Mark Hawthorne and Officer Thompson made their way to where Jo and the sheriff stood.

"I have to follow Tango." Jo shifted her backpack and took a step toward the dog.

Sheriff Porter nodded. "Thompson, you go with Jo." The sheriff turned to Jo. "Good hunting."

Jo gave the sheriff a 'thumbs up" then glanced over at Officer Thompson. "Ready?"

"Yes, ma'am."

Tango barked from the edge of the woods where he stood looking back at them.

"Let's go." Jo started across the courtyard at

a jog with Thompson behind her.

Once they reached the woods, Jo halted beside Tango and motioned for Thompson to stay behind her. "Okay, Tango. We're ready. Go find."

Tango lowered his nose to the ground and started down the path into the woods. The path was wide enough that two people could walk side by side. It wound this way and that, around tall pines and between clumps of shrubby bushes. Ahead of them, Tango halted and barked. Jo hurried to him. A fuzzy brown slipper lay on the path. Jo picked it up. "This must belong to Mr. Hawthorne. It hasn't been here long enough to get dirty." She handed it to Thompson. At least they were on the right trail. Not that she doubted Tango, but it was always nice to have physical proof. "Good boy, Tango. Go find."

Tango kept a steady pace for almost an hour. Approaching a small bend in the trail, Tango stopped and sniffed the air.

Jo halted and watched as Tango cast back and forth across the trail, nose in the air.

"What's he doing?" Thompson's gaze followed Tango while he searched the clearing. "Did he lose the track?"

"He's looking for something." Jo took a deep breath. "Just let him work."

Tango took a step down the trail then halted. He whined and looked back at Jo then trotted off the trail and into the forest.

Jo pulled a roll of plastic trail tape from her backpack and hung a strip on a low branch. The red tape fluttered in the light breeze.

"Let's go." Jo followed Tango with Thompson behind her. She pushed aside scraggly branches and made her way through the low bushes and undergrowth. She couldn't see Tango but could hear him nearby. A fallen tree blocked their path, and they circled it. Tango barked somewhere ahead of them. He had gone farther than she thought. Tango barked again.

"He's found something." Jo and Thompson struggled through brush and soon came to a clearing. Tango looked at them and barked.

There was no Mr. Hawthorne. Just a bare patch of ground covered by loose dirt. "What is it, boy? What'd you find?"

Tango pawed the ground and began digging,

throwing dirt behind him. Jo reached his side and watched him dig. "Oh, shhh...." She grabbed his collar. "Enough, Tango. Good boy."

Thompson stood next to her. "That's not Mr. Hawthorne."

"You have any idea who it is?" Jo put a hand over her nose and shivered.

"Nope. He hasn't been here long though." Thompson keyed the mic on his radio. "This doesn't look like a missing person either."

Jo led Tango across the clearing and offered him water from her backpack while Thompson talked to the sheriff back at the search command center. She shivered again. Tango had been trained for search and rescue along with recovery, but Mom had never let her go on those searches

Thompson strolled over and leaned against a tree. "Sheriff Porter is going to send a team in. I need to wait and meet them here." He glanced at his watch. "He said for you to wait and not go on alone."

"But, Mr. Hawthorne's still..."

"I know. And I understand." He glanced at his watch again. "The sheriff said no way was I to let you go off alone. The person who buried this guy could still be out there nearby."

"But..."

Officer Thompson shook his head.

"Fine. But I'm not happy." Jo glared at Thompson until he walked back to the partially buried body.

Tango sat at the edge of the clearing looking

back at Jo. She patted her leg and called him. He whined and looked toward the ground then back at Jo. She walked over to him and gazed at the dirt. A broken pine branch lay next to a shoe print. "Good boy, Tango. Good boy." Jo pulled her phone from her pocket and selected camera. She took a dollar bill from her wallet and laid it next to the shoe print then took several photos.

Officer Thompson strolled over. "Nice catch, girl. I think you found our bad guy's footprints." He knelt next to the print.

Jo took hold of Tango's collar and led him across the clearing then looked back at Thompson. He still knelt there, his back to Jo. She took a deep breath then stepped into the forest and hurried toward the main trail, Tango at her side.

Chapter Four

Thompson called her name. She ignored him and continued through the brush. She'd probably be in trouble but Mr. Hawthorne still waited to be found, and it was her job to find him. Well, her's and Tango's. Back on the main trail, Jo pulled the lost man's shirt from her backpack and once again presented it to Tango.

"Go find, Tango."

Tango took off down the trail, nose to the ground.

Jo shifted her backpack higher and followed. He trotted around a bend in the trail and disappeared. Before Jo got where she could see him, he barked. An excited, I-found-it, kind of bark. Jo jogged around a clump of scrubby brush. Tango stood next to an elderly man who lay on the ground curled into a tight ball. Tango looked back at her and barked.

"Good boy, Tango." Jo hurried to them and knelt beside the man. Yep, Mr. Hawthorne. A soft moan let her know he was alive.

"Mr. Hawthorne, I'm Jo, and this is Tango. We've been looking for you." She put his slipper back on his foot and wrapped him in a blanket from her backpack. "Now, let's get some help out here and get you back to the center."

Jo keyed her handheld radio. "Command, this is K9 One. We have him. I repeat, we have found the victim."

"K9 One, what is the status of the victim?" Static accompanied Sheriff Porter's reply.

"Command, weak, cold and tired, disoriented. I'm going to need help getting him back."

"Roger, K9 One. I'll have a team come to you. Where are you located?"

Jo gave the sheriff directions then signed off and turned her attention back to Mr. Hawthorne. He wasn't as pale and seemed to be less disoriented. He tried to sit, so Jo helped him lean against the nearest tree.

"I heard voices...tried to find them." Frank pulled the blanket tighter.

"Shhhh... You rest. it's okay, Mr. Hawthorne." She took a bottle of water from her backpack, removed the cap, and handed it to him. "Try to drink this."

"Thank you." his voice quivered almost as much as his hands shook when he handed her the bottle. Tango crept to where Frank sat and then rested his head on the old man's lap. "Call me Frank."

Jo patted Tango on the shoulder and grinned. "Not bad for a day's work, huh Tango?"

Tango lifted his head and stared down the trail, back the way they'd come. "What is it, boy?"

Jo listened and soon heard a low rumble that slowly got louder. Soon a golf cart came into view. Sheriff Porter and a woman in nurse's scrubs sat in the front seat. The cart halted next to them, and the nurse hurried to Frank.

The sheriff slid off the seat and clapped Jo on the back. "Your skinny German Shepherd did a good job." He laughed. "Tell the diva she owes him a steak."

"I think we'll pass. She's going to be angry about that ticket, so I'm gonna let her be." Jo zipped her backpack, slung it over her shoulder. "Did your guys get the remains from the other site?"

He nodded. "They're working on it. It shouldn't take long to figure out who he is." He pulled Jo aside. "I gave instructions for you to stay with Thompson. It could have been dangerous out here alone." He shook his head. "I'm not going to tell your mother this time. But, it better not happen again. Understand?"

Jo nodded. "Yes, sir." Better to humor him. Mom might agree that finding Mr. Hawthorne was the important thing, but she might side with the sheriff. Best to let sleeping dogs lie.

"I'm ready to move Mr. Hawthorne." The nurse stood and looped her stethoscope around her neck.

"Let me get this cart turned around first." Ted looked around. "I'm going to have to unhitch the trailer."

"I'll get it." Jo tossed her pack on the seat and went to the rear of the cart and unhitched the small trailer then turned it around while Sheriff Porter found a wider spot in the trail and turned around. When he returned, he scooted the cart past the trailer and halted.

Once the trailer was hitched, the sheriff carried Frank to the trailer and laid him on a small mattress. Tango jumped up next to him and lay down.

Jo sat on the end of the trailer, her feet dangling off. "I'll ride back here with him and Tango."

Sheriff Porter nodded. "All right. Let's go."

Jo tucked the blanket around Frank then grabbed hold of the cart side. "Better hold on Tango, it's gonna be a bumpy ride."

Chapter Five

The trail began to widen as they neared the living center. Jo leaned over, pulled the blanket up, and put a hand on Frank's shoulder. "Almost there."

Frank fumbled for her hand, held it as tight as he could. "Tell the sheriff. They were arguing. In too deep, couldn't back out now." Frank coughed then shivered. "She insisted he do his job."

The trail gave way to open grass, and the living center came into view. A crowd stood outside waiting for them. Sheriff Porter halted the golf cart in front of the building as the people applauded. Jo slid off the trailer and called Tango to her side.

Tiffany hurried to her father, grabbed his hand, and held it to her face. "Oh, Daddy. I was so worried."

Two orderlies brought a gurney and lifted Frank onto it. As they tightened the straps, Tango trotted over to one of the men and sat. He looked back at Jo and barked. The orderly tried to shoo him away. Tango barked again.

Jo went to him. "Sorry. He's a bit excited." She looked down at Tango and saw the orderlies shoes. Dirt filled the crease around the edge. The same color dirt as from the woods. Jo gazed up at the orderly whose nametag read Tim. "Why did you do it?"

"I don't know what you're talking about. Get your dog away so I can get Mr. Hawthorne inside." Tim pushed the gurney a step toward the doors.

Tango growled then stood.

Tiffany gasped. "Get away, dog. Sheriff, Sheriff!"

She glared at Jo. "I told you that dog was sick; now he's gone mad. Get him away from my father."

The sheriff strode over to them. "What's the problem?"

"That dog's gone mad." Tiffany pointed at Jo. "Make her take it away."

Jo gazed up at Sheriff Porter. "Tango knows who buried the body in the woods." She rubbed her hand down her pant leg. "Frank, err…Mr. Hawthorne said he heard a man and woman arguing and was trying to find them. He heard them talking about having to do a job." Jo pulled her phone from her pocket. "He tried to cover up everything with a broken branch. He missed a footprint though." She pulled up the photos she'd taken. "Tango recognized his scent when he brought the gurney over. Tim is the one who buried the guy we found. He has the same dirt on his shoes."

Tim took a step toward the parking lot, then broke into a run.

Tango looked back at Jo and whined. Jo nodded

and made a sweeping motion with her arm and pointed at Tim as he ran. Tango raced full speed across the grass, launched himself off a bench, and landed on Tim's back. They crashed to the ground. Tango barked furiously as Tim lay there.

Jo and Sheriff Porter ran to where Tim lay. Jo called Tango. He ran to her side and sat. She scratched him behind the ears. "Good boy, Tango."

"She made me do it. Nurse Carlisle, she made me do it. I'll tell you everything." Tim glanced over at Tango. "Just keep that dog away from me."

The sheriff helped Tim to stand, then cuffed him and led him to a nearby cruiser. After getting Tim in the backseat and on his way to jail, Sheriff Porter strolled over to Jo. He knelt in front of Tango and scratched his chest. "You two make a good team. I'll be sure to let your mom know." He stood and smiled. "Now, let's go do the paperwork."

Chapter Six

Monday morning Jo rested her arms on top the half-door and watched Ziva's puppies scarf their breakfast. Purple-collar pup trotted to the door and barked at Jo. She reached over the door and rubbed his head. One day, she'd have a pup of her own, but until then, she could wait. She gave purple-collar pup another pat then strolled out the door.

Diego's truck pulled in and parked. Mom got out of it and strode toward Jo. Jo took a deep breath and

hoped Sheriff Porter kept his word about not telling Mom about disobeying orders. Her mom smiled and pulled Jo into a hug.

"I'm so proud of you." She held Jo by the shoulders at arm's length and looked down at her. "Ted told me you really stepped up and impressed him." She pulled Jo into another hug. "I think it's time you had a pup of your own to train. Maybe that purple-collar boy?

CPSIA information can be obtained
at www.ICGtesting.com
Printed in the USA
LVHW081511030519
616573LV00011B/549/P